First Published in the UK in 2017 by
FORTH BOOKS
www.forthbooks.co.uk

Text copyright ©2017 A.H. Proctor
Cover illustration copyright ©2017 Ed Norton
Illustrations copyright ©2017 P.S. Brooks

ISBN 978-1-909266-11-7 Thumble Tumble and the Ollpheist (PBK)
ISBN 978-1-909266-12-4 Thumble Tumble and the Ollpheist (e-book)

A CIP record of this book is available
from the British Library.

Printed and bound by Bell & Bain Ltd, Glasgow.

For Skye and Kyle, my little bookworms,
and for Jessie, who never stopped believing

Contents

Chapter 1

The Broken Coven

A long time ago, on a tiny island just off the coast of
Scotland, there gathered a coven of witches. This coven
brought together thirteen of the most powerful witches on
Earth. The witches had travelled from some of the most
remote places on the planet, from the vast, freezing cold
plains of Iceland in the North, to the great barren deserts
that straddle the equator.

The witches gathered in secret on this little island
every one hundred years in order to restore the balance of
good and evil.

The coven consisted of six good witches, six dark
witches and the Arbitrator, a witch who was neither good
nor evil. Amongst the dark witches there was an Ice Witch
called Frangelica, a Troll Witch called Tabathay, and a
Night Witch called Mogdred – the most evil and powerful
of all the dark witches.

The fine balance between good and evil had prevailed
throughout the centuries, until one day Mogdred decided
that she wanted to rule over the coven. And so a dangerous

The Witch Council

struggle between good and evil began.

Mogdred used her most evil and cunning powers to turn witch against witch. All those who would not yield to her command were destroyed. Over the years, Mogdred and her followers killed hundreds of good witches and dark forces began to appear on Earth, for when the coven was broken, so too was the balance between good and evil.

As Mogdred's powers grew, so did her cloak of darkness. It engulfed everything that lay before it. If she was not stopped, she would soon cover the whole world in a blanket of evil, and good would be gone… forever! The elders called an important gathering of the Witch Council, where it was unanimously agreed that Mogdred had to be stopped. The Witch Council selected, Isla, Bessie and Lizzie – three sisters from the Isle of Arran, the very place the coven had chosen for their emergency meeting – to stand against Mogdred and put an end to her tyranny.

Even though she had held the power of the Protector since she was a child, Lizzie had never been called to appear before the elders before. She wondered what was in store for her. As she walked slowly along the dark corridor that ran through the Witch Council dungeons, the dim, flickering light that came from the sparsely hung candles suddenly reminded her of the night she had gained her special Protector powers. She had been sitting at her mother's bedside, sobbing into her little white handkerchief. Her mother's time on Earth was coming to an end. At the precise moment she passed away, the silver necklace she wore around her neck glowed with a light so bright that it hurt Lizzie's eyes, but even so, Lizzie saw the light jump from the necklace onto the handkerchief she was clutching in her hand. Then the light was gone. That was how her mother's powers had been transferred to her.

A witch's amulet is usually a piece of jewellery, but in fact it can be anything, and Lizzie's amulet was the little white handkerchief she now wore tied around her wrist. The amulet is only a physical object to hold the power – the source of the power comes from within the witch herself, from her very soul, and can only be passed from mother to daughter at the moment of the mother's death.

Lizzie was the youngest of the three sisters. Her two elder sisters had been born a long time before her, with a gap of over a hundred years between them and her. As a Protector of the coven, their mother had been given great powers by the coven to help her defend it against its enemies. The powers bestowed upon a Protector come from every species of witch, so that the Protector possesses an accumulation of the powers of every witch on Earth. The force is so strong that it cannot be contained within one witch's body, and is therefore held within the Protector's amulet.

Lizzie nervously twisted her left hand around the handkerchief tied onto her right wrist as the gnarled wooden doors at the end of the corridor came into view. At her approach, the massive iron bolt slid out and dropped to the floor with a bang so loud, she thought it had shattered. The doors to the Witch Council chamber then swung open, revealing an oval-shaped room at the centre of which was an oval table.

At the head of the table sat a witch holding a wand tipped with a gleaming glass globe that Lizzie found it hard to take her eyes off. Her silvery-grey hair trailed right down to the ground and she was dressed in silver robes that matched her complexion. From stories she had heard from Bessie and Isla, Lizzie recognised her instantly: this must be the Arbitrator. To the Arbitrator's left sat six witches, each more beautiful than the last. And to her right sat five of the most foul looking creatures imaginable. There was one empty seat at the table.

As Lizzie stepped through the doorway, one of the fearsomely ugly witches slithered off its chair and levitated towards her.

"So you are the so-called Protector," it hissed in her face.

Lizzie recoiled in alarm.

"That's enough, Tabathay," said the Arbitrator, glaring at the cloaked figure. She paused until it had slithered back into its seat.

"Please come forward, Lizzie," she continued, in a tone that was warm but firm. "Do you know why we have called you here?"

"No. I'm guessing it has something to do with Mogdred."

"Your guess is correct. As you know, the Protector's role is to ensure the future of the coven. And we must now call on you to do just that."

"She's no match for Mogdred," screeched an Ice Witch, sending a chilling breeze through the room.

"I know Lizzie is not fully trained yet, Frangelica," replied the Arbitrator. "But as you know, Mogdred's powers are growing daily. If we do not act soon, she may become too strong for us to stop."

"Then perhaps we shouldn't try to stop her," Frangelica retorted. Her complexion was so pale that her eyes glistened from the light reflected from her icy façade and the veins on her forehead stood out like blue scars.

One of the beautiful witches rose gracefully. Sweeping her luxuriant golden locks back over her shoulders, she slammed her hands flat on the table. Lizzie leapt back even further this time. The unexpected outburst had given her an even bigger fright than the slithering creature had!

"I know you would prefer to see the world under a sheet of ice, Frangelica. But if Mogdred doesn't stop, there will be no world left for you to freeze. Don't you understand?" she shouted. "If Mogdred's evil continues to grow, she will destroy us all – good and evil."

"Order!" the Arbitrator interjected, motioning the elegant witch to sit down.

"Lizzie will not be alone in her quest. As I understand it, Lizzie, your sisters have the power of Spellbinder and Alchemist, do they not?"

"Yes, they do," Lizzie nodded.

"Bessie is a brilliant Spellbinder who can cast any

spell from the Book of Enchantment, and Isla can create a potion just by thinking about what it does."

"Then it is agreed," announced the Arbitrator. "Lizzie will battle Mogdred with the help of her two sisters, Bessie and Isla, right here on Arran."

"And just how do you propose getting Mogdred to come here – to the very heart of the coven?" hissed Tabathay. Tabathay was a Witch Troll. She had a long thin body and her head was gigantic, which was ironic as Witch Trolls are usually all brawn with very little brain!

"We shall offer up a prize – a prize so great, she cannot resist!"

The Arbitrator said decisively. Raising her wand above her head, she shouted "Glanceoso!" Lizzie ducked as the globe detached from the tip of the wand and whizzed over her head. It shattered against the wall, but instead of the broken pieces of glass falling to the floor, they formed into a huge mirror that was magically suspended on the wall.

"The All Seeing Globe," smiled the Arbitrator.

"But how will Mogdred find out that Lizzie has the globe?" Tabathay snarled.

"I'm sure we can rely on someone in this very room to betray us," replied the Arbitrator, raising an eyebrow in the direction of Tabathay and Frangelica.

Chapter 2

The Ring

Isla was standing on the road at the edge of the Light and Dark Forest when she felt the night air turn icy cold. She looked up to see a huge black cloud billowing across the sky, rubbing out the stars as it spread. She gently lifted her wand in the air and waved it around, as though drawing a picture. A second later, the hoot of a snowy owl rang through the trees and Isla hopped onto her broom and disappeared into the forest.

"That's the signal," Lizzie whispered to Bessie.

"Mogdred must have taken the bait. She's here to get the All Seeing Globe."

Lizzie and Bessie were in a small clearing in the centre of the forest, where they had been waiting for hours to hear the hoot of a snowy owl, the signal from Isla that the Night Witches had arrived!

"Ok, you know what to do," Bessie said, hugging her sister. "But please be careful... Mogdred is crafty, and very dangerous!"

"I'll be fine," said Lizzie. Breaking free from her

sister's bear hug, she turned and headed through the trees towards the road at the end of the forest.

Bessie was just about to fly up into the sky when she thought she heard a twig snap behind her.

She sat motionless in the clearing, her legs hitched over her broom, hovering just a couple of inches off the ground.

After a few seconds she tilted sideways, pushed off with her foot and flew up to the treetops – only to come hurtling back towards the ground like a peregrine falcon.

"Revealeo!" she commanded, pointing her wand towards two tall trees at the side of the clearing.

Immediately, the trees appeared to come to life!

Two scrawny arms shot out of the tree on Bessie's left. Then a long bony leg appeared, followed by a giant bulbous head and a second leg. The creature then peeled itself away from the tree. It was covered in bark from head to toe and wore a vacant expression on its face.

An almost identical creature emerged from the tree on Bessie's right – the only difference being that this one was missing a foot.

"Hello, gents," she said in a wary voice. "Have you been spying on us?"

The two Tree Trolls stared at one another for a moment, then answered at the same time.

"No, Bessie, we were just resting in the trees," spluttered Ugg.

"No, Bessie, we were just trying to spot butterflies," gasped Ogg.

The Tree Troll twins then both reversed their answers!

"Hmm… I see," said Bessie, in a dubious tone.

Bessie had not seen a Tree Troll for years. In fact, the

14

last time she had seen one was when Mogdred started her war on the coven. Mogdred had recruited the Tree Trolls as spies, and ever since they had remained hidden so that they could snoop on her enemies.

"What we meant to say is that we were resting in the trees, butterfly spotting," lied Ugg, edging his way towards Bessie.

"And what I meant to say was Weedious Stableus!" boomed Bessie, pointing her wand at the Trolls' feet. Long green strands of weeds started popping out from between their toes and began rooting themselves into the ground.

Ugg and Ogg lurched forward, grasping at Bessie's wand, but their feet were stuck fast to the ground and they both fell flat on their faces.

The Tree Trolls twisted their heads round and each broke into a mean, crooked smile.

"You're too late," they sniggered in chorus. "Mogdred already knows your plan."

At these words, Bessie felt deeply alarmed. There was no time to deal with the Tree Trolls properly. She hastily jumped onto her broom and took to the skies.

Mogdred had just landed her broom in another part of the forest and was waiting impatiently for her lazy daughters, Sloth and Gretch.

Like all Night Witches Mogdred had black skin, hair, teeth and nails, making it practically impossible to see her in the dark.

Night Witches can see through their thin black eyelids and so, to enhance their concealment, they habitually keep their eyes closed. The only sure way to detect one is from its foul breath, which smells like a rancid sewer.

However, if they open their eyes Night Witches can

be seen in the darkness straight away, because their eyes are white with no pupil in the centre. Even the slightest glimmer of light is blinding to them. This was why they always launch an attack under the cover of darkness.

Mogdred's daughters, Sloth and Gretch, were obese and very lazy. Neither had wanted to fly all the way to the Isle of Arran, and they were still moaning about how long it was since they had last eaten when they landed on the island. They were so busy grumbling that they had set down a mile off course, on the wrong side of the forest!

"I can't believe we've had to fly all the way here for a stupid globe," grunted Sloth.

"I know," snorted Gretch, as they waddled in single file through the trees, like two hippos trying to squeeze through a narrow tunnel.

Suddenly, Gretch stopped in her tracks. Sloth bounced off her bottom.

Before Gretch could even lift a finger, Lizzie flicked her wrist and sent the sisters flying up into the air.

Sloth landed with such a thud that she left an imprint of her huge bottom on the ground where she fell. Gretch hit a tree, and the force of the impact caused it to snap in two, with the top half landing right on her head.

Sloth sat up and pointed her long black finger towards Lizzie, but she was too slow. Lizzie was already twirling her finger around in a circle and smiling.

Next thing she knew, Sloth was spinning round and round, up in the air, with a rope wrapping itself around her feet. The rope then bound her hands and wrapped itself around her face like a gag, before untying and dropping her back onto the ground, where she landed with another bone-shaking thud.

Lizzie now turned her attention to Gretch, who had climbed out from under the tree and was now casting a Death Curse towards her. Lizzie ducked down as the spell shot out of Gretch's long black finger and went right over the top of her head like a thunderbolt.

Hiding in the foliage, exactly where her spies the Tree Trolls had said Lizzie would be, Mogdred surveyed the battle between Lizzie and her daughters from the cover of dark green leaves. She waited patiently until Lizzie's back was turned before casting her most deadly spell.

The Death Bolt hit Lizzie in the middle of her back.

"No!" screamed Isla, swooping down towards Mogdred, carrying a small pink vial in her hand. Mogdred fired another Death Bolt from her wand, but this time it missed.

Isla threw the vial at Mogdred's head. It hit her right between the eyes and shattered into tiny pieces, allowing the thick brown liquid it contained to pour over Mogdred's face.

Just at that moment Bessie appeared from the dark clouds above.

She was late… too late!

Tears poured down her face and she began chanting. Her spell tore through the black clouds like a tornado, pulling them apart. Shards of light started to penetrate the darkness as the sun began to rise on the horizon. Within seconds, bright sunlight penetrated the entire forest.

Mogdred howled in pain as the potion Isla had thrown on her face began to erode the thin layer of skin covering her eyes. In moments, the skin disappeared completely, exposing her vulnerable white eyes to the full force of the sun.

Bessie and Isla flew down to Lizzie's side where she

17

lay on the ground. Shards of pink glass from the broken vial surrounded her like a circle of rose petals. She could barely breathe and every word she spoke was weaker than the last.

"Don't be sad, my sisters," Lizzie murmured. "Good has prevailed."

She dropped the All Seeing Globe into Isla's hand.

Forcing the words up from her failing lungs, with almost no sound at all she mouthed, "But I fear this battle is not over yet."

A single tear rolled down her cheek and landed on a fragment of broken glass. As it did so, a little white light hovered up from the handkerchief on her wrist and wrapped itself around the teardrop.

Lizzie was gone.

Bessie quickly took out her wand and cast a forging spell, turning the piece of glass into a small ring, which she carefully placed in her pocket.

That done, Bessie rounded on the Night Witches with

The amulet ring

redoubled fury. Gretch was now holding Mogdred under her arms, trying to haul her through the trees with her feet dragging behind her through the undergrowth. They were heading into the darkest part of the forest, towards the swamps where she knew they could escape.

Bessie pushed her hand straight up to the sky, pointing her finger towards the heavens, and then, with all her might she bellowed, "Stillamomentum!"

This spell, known as a 'pausing spell', stops time for a few seconds. It is one of the most difficult spells to conjure, and only a few witches in the whole world are able to do it.

As soon as Bessie had uttered the pausing spell, the leaves falling from the trees froze exactly where they had been drifting in the air. Gretch's size eleven feet were floating three inches off the ground, with Mogdred's body draped over her arms, as time stood still. The spell also immobilised Isla, leaving her standing motionless in the sunlight, holding the precious All Seeing Globe in her hand.

Casting the spell had taken every last drop of Bessie's energy. Her arm dropped back down to her side and her head flopped forward, tilting to one side. She was so drained, all she could do was watch Sloth, surrounded by her shielding spell, pull the statue-like bodies of Mogdred and Gretch onto her broom.

She then grabbed the globe from Isla's hand, before flying deep into the forest.

The Night Witches had vanished... for now!

Chapter 3

The Good Witches

"Toe of toad, slime of snail, drop them in and stir it well. Sprig of heather, buzzard's feather, add the lot then have a smell. Not quite right? Add pinch of night. Then snot of newt and an old black boot."

"Ah, perfect," said Isla as she sniffed the aroma wafting up from her cauldron.

Isla was making her famous Scoffalicious Chocolate. At one hundred and fifty-nine years old, she was the oldest witch on the Isle of Arran. She had silver wispy hair, grey eyes, and a thin face, but she still looked pretty and young. One thing about witches is that although they look slightly older as they age, they don't change much physically. A witch can live to well over two hundred years old and still be as fit as a human aged twenty! But one thing that age does affect in a witch is height. Isla used to be almost six feet tall as a young witch, but over the years she had shrunk down to barely five feet tall. Isla always wore the same long purple dress, and now she often tripped over the hem when she walked. As she had never had it taken up over the years, it was now a foot too long for her. On her head she always sported a small green pointy hat that glistened so much it looked as though it was covered in green glitter. In reality, it was covered in green sparkly dust from making her many unusual potions.

Scoffalicious Chocolate is, of course, magic chocolate. It tastes just like the favourite food of the person eating it, so if you love raspberry ice-cream topped with candy-floss, Scoffalicious Chocolate will taste to you just like raspberry ice-cream and candy-floss. Even if you like eating something really gross, like slugs wrapped in lettuce leaves, that's the flavour Scoffalicious Chocolate will be for you... yuk!

Isla was busy making a giant batch of Scoffalicious Chocolate for King Rohan. It was the day of Great Games at Lochranza Castle, and the King of the Deer Folk had ordered ten gallons of Scoffalicious Chocolate to serve along with honey wine and berries for after the games.

Isla's huge cauldron was filled to the brim with Scoffalicious Chocolate. The cauldron had been simmering on the stove for hours as she made batch after batch, each of which had been poured into pots, ready to go.

At first glance, the kitchen appeared to be really small. The stove stood right in the centre of the room, with two large fridges against the walls on either side of it. There were various cupboards, sinks and chopping boards and the usual array of utensils dotted around. But some very peculiar objects also shared the kitchen alongside the cooking equipment. For one thing, in the corner under the window there was an odd looking trampoline. And even this was not as unexpected as the tightrope stretched from one wall to the other, right above the stove. It was a very strange looking kitchen indeed, and much bigger than it seemed.

Blue smoke was billowing up from the chocolate bubbling on the stove. The smoke wafted up the chimney and out into the cold morning air. There was often coloured smoke or sparks coming out of Auntie Isla's chimney. If it wasn't coming from Isla's peculiar cooking, it would be from one of Auntie Bessie's wacky spells.

The smoke looked like blue shoelaces as it crept back down the chimney and began twisting and spiralling around the kitchen. It passed through the open door and up to the top of the stairs, where the shoelaces of smoke wrapped themselves around a silver door knob shaped like a starfish. It then moved to the tiny crack that ran all the way around the bedroom door, which never quite closed properly. The blue smoke seeped into the bedroom and over to the sleeping figure in the bed. It drifted up the little girl's nostrils, waking her from the most amazing dream. In her dream, Thumble Tumble had been eating the most delicious juicy chocolate-covered strawberries. No doubt the aroma of her aunt's Scoffalicious Chocolate percolating through the cottage had something to do with it!

Thumble Tumble lived in a little white cottage on the Isle of Arran with her Auntie Isla and her Auntie Bessie. She was eight years old and had lived with her aunts for as long as she could remember. Thumble Tumble had shoulder-length curly blonde hair, light blue eyes and pale white skin. She was very small for her age – so small, that her hat was almost as tall as she was. Like all witch's hats, her hat was tall and pointed. But rather than being black or grey, it was bright blue, and in the winter she would put a pom-pom on the point and go sledging on her broom.

Thumble Tumble's favourite colour was pink and she would always have something pink on – even if it was just her little pink ring. She had had this ring ever since she was a baby. It was the only thing she possessed from her mother, so it was very precious to her. The ring was made of glass with a tiny glass teardrop as the centrepiece, and it now only fitted her pinkie finger.

The smell of the Scoffalicious Chocolate was irresistible. Thumble Tumble couldn't stay in bed a moment longer. She sprang out of bed and rushed downstairs to the kitchen, almost standing on poor Flopsy as she ran out of the bedroom door. Flopsy was Thumble Tumble's cat and as you would expect from a girl who loves pink, Flopsy's fur was bright pink and really soft and fluffy. Other than being pink, Flopsy was just like any other cat: she liked milk, sleep and being stroked, and that was about that.

Thumble Tumble burst through the kitchen door to find her Auntie Isla pouring the last batch of Scoffalicious Chocolate into pots and placing them by the door.

"Am I in time?" Thumble Tumble asked anxiously.

"Of course you are," said Isla, handing her niece a big wooden spoon covered in Scoffalicious Chocolate.

After she had licked every last drop of chocolate off the spoon, Thumble Tumble finally said good morning to her Auntie Bessie, who had come into the kitchen and was now standing over the stove trying to cast a spell to get the cauldron to clean itself.

"Abrika, hocus and twiddle e dee…"

Nothing was happening!

Bessie was brilliant at casting spells, but she was a

bit wacky, even by witch standards, and sometimes this would carry into her spells. One time, when she was casting a 'freezing' spell on a Tree Troll to keep it still, instead of freezing the Tree Troll, her spell had cast a sheet of ice over the whole of Arran, and it was freezing cold for a whole week in the middle of summer!

"Alacazam! Alacazum! Make the dirt on this cauldron disappear with the touch of my thumb."

She touched the cauldron with her thumb and suddenly there was a puff of green smoke.

Then, plop, plop, two legs popped out of the bottom of the cauldron. The legs were really skinny, like twigs, with huge feet wearing stripy red and white socks and running shoes. Then, whoosh… the cauldron got up and ran straight out of the front door!

This was not at all what Bessie had in mind, but at least the dirt had disappeared.

"I'll head out later to find the cauldron. Hopefully before anyone sees it," she said with a sigh.

The sprinting cauldron

Bessie had been an exceptionally beautiful witch in her youth, and even at the age of one hundred and twenty-two she was still gorgeous, with short spiky jet-black hair, dark brown eyes and rosy lips. She always wore a rainbow coloured dress that went all the way down to her toes. It was a patchwork of different textures – cloth, leaves, fur, and wool. Bessie was regarded as a rather unconventional witch. She never wore shoes and instead of having a cat as her companion, she had a bat called Podi.

Podi, a stinky little bat who did not like washing, flying or walking, lived under Bessie's hat. This way he could travel wherever she did without ever having to stretch his wings – which he also didn't like doing if he could help it.

Bessie had found him one day when she was scouring the beach looking for Raven Shells to make a Dragon Cake. The purple-black shells are perfect for decorating Dragon Cakes, as they look just like dragon scales. She was collecting the shells in a small cauldron. When it was just about full, Bessie picked it up and hopped onto her broom to leave, when out of the corner of her eye she noticed what she thought was a small shell twitching at the edge of the water. She went over to investigate, but instead of a Raven Shell she found a tiny little bat covered in goo. The little guy was just about dead when she picked him up and placed him under her hat and they have been inseparable ever since.

"Who is all this Scoffalicious Chocolate for?" asked Thumble Tumble.

"It's for King Rohan," replied Isla. "It's part of the feast that will take place after the Great Games today."

King Rohan was the King of the Deer Folk. Half human, half deer, the Deer Folk live in the grounds of

Lochranza Castle. Deer Folk are very powerful creatures with human torsos and the legs and antlers of a deer. They are toned and muscular, and have the strength of ten human men when they are fully grown.

Thumble Tumble had met King Rohan once, a long time ago when she was very little. Her memory of meeting him was very foggy. She thought it must have been at night, as it was dark. She had a clearer memory of a big circle of scary looking witches flying on their brooms around her head, and of men with horns and horses' legs firing silver arrows from huge bows at the circle of witches. She had thought they were some sort of devils with horns. Later, her aunts told her that the strange looking men were in fact Deer Folk.

Thumble Tumble had heard all about the Deer Folk and their Great Games from her aunts. The games sounded awesome, and she was desperate to see them for herself. But every year she asked to go, she had been told that it was too dangerous and that she was too little to go. She knew it would be the same answer this year if she asked. So instead, she thought of a plan.

"Can I help you deliver the Scoffalicious Chocolate to the castle?" she asked her Auntie Isla in an innocent tone.

Isla knew that Thumble Tumble was only offering to deliver the chocolate in an attempt to sneak in and see the games. But Isla also knew that the games wouldn't start for hours. What Thumble Tumble didn't know was that the first event didn't kick off until sunset. Isla was certain there was no chance of her little niece sneaking into the games this early in the morning.

"Of course you can deliver the chocolate," smiled Isla. "Just remember to be home before dark," and she bent down and kissed Thumble Tumble on the forehead.

Yes, thought Thumble Tumble. *The Plan has worked.*

She raced back upstairs to her bedroom, which was under the eaves of the little white cottage. The cottage sat halfway along a quiet road that had a very peaceful feeling about it, as very few passers-by ever came this way. There were only five cottages on the road, which ran down to a stretch of stony beach from which you could see the beautiful Holy Isle across the sea. At the top of the road was Blakk Cemetery, where there were lots of old headstones with the names of humans who had died a long time ago. The cemetery was supposedly haunted, but Thumble Tumble had never been tempted to go in at night to find out if this was true.

The little white cottage had two chimneys from which there was always some bright-coloured smoke or sparks shooting into the sky. This was a bit strange as there was only one fire inside the cottage, which was under the stove in the kitchen, and so no one could ever work out where the other chimney smoke was coming from!

The cottage had a black wooden door with a ship's porthole right in the middle of it. You couldn't see into the cottage through the porthole from the outside, but from the inside it acted like a magnifying glass, making the face of anyone knocking on the door look gigantic! Their eye would look as though it was the full size of the porthole if they tried to peer in.

Thumble Tumble found this quite scary sometimes, especially if a little housefly was hovering at the porthole, as from inside the cottage it looked like a monster fly trying to get inside to gobble her up! Although the door was made of wood, if you licked it, it tasted like liquorice

27

and Thumble Tumble couldn't resist having a lick of the door every time she came in.

The cottage had two small square windows that popped out of the roof. One window looked out from Thumble Tumble's bedroom and the other from Auntie Bessie's room. Both rooms looked tiny from outside, and unlike the kitchen, they really were. Their coved ceilings slanted right down from the centre to the floor, like a tent.

Thumble Tumble was small enough to just about stand up in her room without banging her head. But Bessie was forever banging her hat off of the slanted ceiling, which would of course wake up poor Podi from his preferred state of sleep. "Ouch!" you would hear Podi squeal from under Bessie's hat first thing in the morning. This was because Bessie would always forget to duck as she stepped out of bed. The commotion acted like an alarm clock for Thumble Tumble and Isla, as Bessie woke up every morning at 7am sharp with a loud "Ouch!" from Podi.

Chapter 4

Lochs, Castles and Rumours

Thumble Tumble got dressed into a pink dress with a big silver star on the front, stripy green and yellow tights, pink Converse trainers and a bright blue hat, which she pulled down to just above her eyebrows. It was February and there was snow still lying on the ground outside, so Thumble Tumble attached a big pink woolly pom-pom to the point of her hat.

She went back downstairs and got her broom from the broom cupboard under the stairs along with her red wool cloak, then headed into the kitchen and started loading the pots of Scoffalicious Chocolate into the little basket attached to the back of her broom.

The basket looked like the sort you would attach to the front of a bicycle, but it was a magic basket, so it could carry the equivalent of twenty full shopping bags. Into the basket, she loaded all twelve pots of Scoffalicious Chocolate, a strawberry jam sandwich, a bottle of water and two juicy green apples, then rolled up an old picnic blanket and squashed it on top.

"I'm off," she shouted to her aunts, and hopped onto her broom.

"Remember to be back before dark," Auntie Isla called back, but before she could say another word, Thumble Tumble had disappeared through the porthole in the front door.

The porthole was a magical porthole that opened as soon as it detected a good witch on a broom, either outside or inside the cottage. The glass evaporated into thin air, and the porthole would then expand to the full size of the door. As soon as the good witch had entered or left the cottage, the porthole would shrink back to its normal size and the glass would reappear, sealing it tight shut. On the other hand, if the porthole detected a dark witch, it would automatically place a protective enchantment over the cottage and trigger a fireworks display of sparks and showers of red and gold flames, a warning sign that could be seen for miles around.

Thumble Tumble flew out into the cold winter air, soaring so high she could never be spotted by humans below. The code of witches, both good and evil, is that they never let humans see them – unless it is absolutely necessary. For good witches, this is usually when they are saving a human from some fiendish creature trying to scoff them. And for evil witches – well, they are usually the fiendish creature!

As an extra precaution especially during the day, just below Thumble Tumble's broom there constantly floated a little white cloud, so that if a human did happen to look up, all they would see was a little cloud and not a witch with a pink pom-pommed hat, flying around on a broom!

As Thumble Tumble flew north towards Lochranza

Castle, she gazed down at the snow-covered cottages below. The route to the castle was along a straight road which followed the shoreline all the way to the village of Sannox, then cut inland through the Giant Hills to Lochranza. Thumble Tumble followed the road until she came to the Pony Woods, where she decided to take a little detour so that she could skim through the snow-capped trees. She loved flying through the woods in winter. She would whizz in and out among the leafless trees, watching sparkling swirls of ice particles fall to the ground as she sped through the bare branches.

After twenty minutes of broom-slaloming, she flew back out of the woods and followed the road again, all the way to Lochranza Castle.

From the outside, the castle looked like an old ruin. Three of its four grey turrets were crumbling away from decades of wind and rain beating against them. The high walls that ran between the turrets, making a perfect square around the internal courtyard, were also falling away in parts from hundreds of years of weather erosion. In contrast, the huge black wrought iron entrance gates were in perfect condition with no rusty bits or holes. In fact, with their fearsome rows of sharp spikes all the way along the top and bottom, the entrance gates looked brand new – it was as if they had just been designed to look five hundred years old!

The castle was apparently so ruinous, people sometimes thought it would be easy to get into, but in fact the opposite was the case. There really was no way in or out other than through the entrance gates. Even the most eroded parts of the walls were still to the height of two giants, one standing on the other's shoulders, and no one had ever managed to climb in.

The castle was also well protected from intruders trying to fly in from the skies above: Deer Folk lay in wait, hidden in the turrets, their huge wooden bows charged and ready to fire. Their solid silver arrows could bring down intruders hundreds of feet above the castle, effectively stopping anything flying above the castle.

The third castle defence was particularly ingenious, and mainly intended to keep humans away! It was put there by a wizard who took refuge at Lochranza Castle one Halloween after being chased there by an angry mob of humans who thought he was a witch (which technically he was, but a male witch). He cast a spell that put a border of hypnotic gas all the way around the castle. The gas is invisible and has no smell, so humans don't even know they are breathing it in. But when they take a breath close to the perimeter of the castle, the hypnotic effects of the gas play tricks with their minds, making them believe all they can see is a tumbledown old ruin. This is the reason why humans rarely if ever see a Deer Folk, and if they do, they just think they have seen a deer, and that their eyes are playing tricks on them!

Lochranza Castle sits on the banks of Domhain Loch. The loch is as black as night and when you look into the water what you see is your own reflection looking back at you. It's as though you are looking at a photograph of yourself that's been printed onto shiny black glass. The loch is impenetrable to the naked eye, and so black that no one dares puts their hand in... just in case!

There are many stories about the loch, stretching back centuries. Some tell of a hideous four-headed sea creature called the Ollpheist. The monster is supposed to live at the bottom of the loch, five hundred miles below the surface. No one really knows how deep the loch actually is, because no one who has gone in to find out has ever returned. Rumour has it that the Ollpheist has four long necks, each with a different head, one with twenty eyes and pincers like a giant spider and the second with three black horns and razor sharp teeth. The third is said to be the head of a cyclops with one eye right in the centre of its forehead, and the fourth, the most deadly of all, is a Devil Ogre, with fangs that carry a poisonous venom.

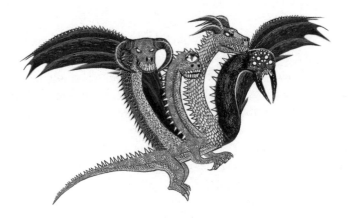

The four-headed Ollpheist

Chapter 5

Rhino Dust

Thumble Tumble carefully laid her broom flat on the ground, unloaded the twelve pots of Scoffalicious Chocolate and stacked them up beside the iron gates of Lochranza Castle. She ran her fingers along the bars of the gates, gently tapping each one as she did so. (This is, of course, the polite way to knock on the door of an enchanted castle.) There was no answer. Thumble Tumble ran her fingers along the bars again, this time tapping each one just a little bit harder.

Still nothing!

From the outside, the castle looked completely deserted – but then it would, to anyone affected by the hypnotic gas. Thumble Tumble thought she must be too early, it was only nine o'clock in the morning after all, and Deer Folk are not known as early risers.

Thumble Tumble decided to wait for the Deer Folk to wake up rather than just leaving the twelve pots of Scoffalicious Chocolate outside the gates – if she did that, she'd never manage to sneak into the Games.

She got out her picnic blanket from the basket that was attached to her broom and laid it out flat on the bank of the loch, close to the castle entrance. Luckily it was warmer here than it had been back at the little white cottage, which meant there was no snow on the ground.

The blanket was covered in dust and when Thumble Tumble spread it out there was cough and a splutter. Not from her, it was the blanket, coughing and spluttering from its own dust!

Thumble Tumble picked it up and gave it a good shake, then laid it back on the ground. But as soon as she had flattened it out, the blanket started crumpling up. Then it began twitching and popping. Finally, it flew up into the air and shook itself frantically, before falling back to the ground.

It was now clear of dust, and perfectly smooth and flat. In the middle of the blanket, there was a green plastic table and a green plastic chair. On top of the table there was a cup, a plate and a set of shiny cutlery. There was also a huge book sitting on the table, with the title 'HOMEWORK' in capital letters blazoned across the cover.

Thumble Tumble plonked herself into the chair and looked at the book. The book opened by itself and announced in a piercing, high-pitched voice, "Today's lesson is arithmetic, and how we use numbers in everyday spells." The book then launched into a series of spells using numbers, starting with the levitating spell.

For this spell you have to know the exact weight of the object you are trying to lift. If you underestimate the weight, the object will be too heavy and you won't be able to move it. If you overestimate its weight, you could send the object up into the sky, beyond the clouds.

This had been done in the past, by none other than Thumble Tumble's Auntie Bessie. As a young student, Bessie used the levitating spell on a pair of shoes – her own shoes! She sent them so high into the sky that they ended up in space, and that's where they've been for the past one hundred years, orbiting Earth. Since that day, she has always gone barefoot.

After three long hours of lessons, and no answer at the castle gates, Thumble Tumble decided it was time for lunch. She went back into the basket attached to her broom and got out her strawberry jam sandwiches, water and apples. As she was putting them down on the table, one of the apples dropped onto the ground and rolled straight into the loch.

Oh rubbish, thought Thumble Tumble. *I'll never get that back.*

Then, from out of the loch, the apple flew through the air and landed on the pink woolly pom-pom on the top of her hat.

Thumble Tumble wasn't sure what to do. She had heard the stories of the terrible sea creature that lived at the bottom of the loch, the Ollpheist!

She was still deciding whether to make a run for it on foot, or take flight on her broom, when the apple fell off her hat and rolled straight back into the loch.

Two seconds later, the apple came hurtling back out of the loch and this time hit her right on the nose. Thumble Tumble acted instinctively. She picked up the apple and threw it with all her might back into the loch. *No one smashes me on the nose with an apple and gets away with it*, she thought. Then she remembered about the

36

hideous creature in the loch, and gulped. But instead of a four-headed monster coming out of the loch, the apple appeared again! This time it landed on the plate on the table that stood on the blanket.

Thumble Tumble was so engrossed with the flying apple that she hadn't noticed she had company, in the form of a nineteen foot tall giant! Rhino was a Spike Back giant. Spike Back giants live in the hills that surround Lochranza Castle. They rarely come down from the hills, as they don't like being shot at by the Deer Folk who live in the castle. And like everyone else, they had heard of the Ollpheist – the monster that lived in the loch — and did not want to end up as its dinner!

As their name suggests, Spike Back giants have spikes that run all the way down their backs from the neck to the base of the spine. The spikes look a bit like rhinoceros horns and that's why they get the nickname 'Rhino'. They are ugly creatures, with green skin that resembles rhinoceros hide with its thick wrinkly texture. They have black beady eyes and lips that roll inside their mouth. This is because they don't have any front teeth, only molars at the back of their mouths. When they see an unsuspecting victim, they usually grab them by the feet and suck them like a lollipop, before popping them into their mouths and chewing them up with their back teeth.

Rhino hadn't planned to come down to the castle today. He had been minding his own business, lying asleep under a tree high up in the hills, when he had been rudely woken up by a huge dollop of dust landing on his face. The dust got up his nose and made his eyes red and itchy. It nearly choked him. He got up to wipe the dust out of his eyes, but this made him start to sneeze. He sneezed so much that he completely lost his balance and rolled all the way down the hill. He only stopped when he banged into the castle gates – which was just as well for him, as a few feet more and he would have been in the loch.

Witches are not high up on the list of favourite food for Spike Back giants. Witches are usually fairly small, but this witch was particularly small. And, Spike Back giants don't have any tastebuds, so they're not really interested in the flavour of their meal, more just the quantity! Nonetheless, Rhino was pretty hungry and a small snack between meals would do him no harm at all, or so he thought.

Thumble Tumble picked up the apple from her plate, spun round and lobbed it straight into Rhino's left eye, which was already red and swollen from all the dust.

She had heard the Spike Back giant tiptoeing up behind her. At nineteen foot tall and weighing the same as a truck, Rhino didn't really sneak up on anyone!

Rhino let out a scream that echoed for miles. He lunged forward to grab Thumble Tumble, but he was still so dizzy from rolling down the hill that all he managed to grab was a handful of air.

Thumble Tumble looked around for her broom. It was still lying in front of the castle gates – right behind Rhino.

There was nowhere for her to go and Rhino knew it.

"Decisions, decisions, my dear," he mumbled through the gap in his lips. "Would you prefer to be eaten by me, or by the Ollpheist?" He paused. "Probably better the devil you know!" he added with a slurp of anticipation.

Thumble Tumble started to walk backwards towards the loch. She wasn't sure how far she could go without ending up in the water, but she certainly wasn't just going to walk straight into Rhino's eager mouth.

Before she realised what she had done, Thumble Tumble started to rise up into the air. It still felt like the ground beneath her feet, but when she looked down it wasn't grass she was standing on anymore, it was seaweed. She fell to her knees with the force of the air pushing down against her as she rose high up into the sky. Whatever this creature was, it didn't have four heads, only one – and she was standing right on top of it.

Thumble Tumble had walked backwards into the loch, and straight onto the head of the Ollpheist!

The creature was soaring up into the sky. It had huge

Thumble Tumble is raised up on the creature's head

wings and a tail that had a pointed tip the shape of an arrow-head.

There was seaweed draped over its head, so Thumble Tumble couldn't see what the hideous monster actually looked like.

The Ollpheist circled once over the castle, then flew straight towards Rhino. Just before it reached him, it opened its huge jaws and sprayed out a torrent of water. The force of the water lifted Rhino off his feet and smashed him against the castle gates. He banged his head off the huge iron gates and sank to the ground in a heap.

The Ollpheist flew back up into the air and started to circle the castle for a second time. Rhino clambered to his feet and ran towards the hills. Too late. The monster came at him from behind this time, with another massive jet of water which pushed Rhino face-first into the ground and dragged him for twenty yards. Rhino was sure that next time the creature would be coming in for the kill. He mustered every bit of energy to get to his feet, then ran as fast as he'd ever run in his entire life before. He could barely catch a breath as he made off, his chest pounding and the muscles in his legs burning. Rhino did not look back once, and did not stop until he was safe back in the hills, where he finally drew breath and collapsed in a heap – relieved still to be alive.

Chapter 6

Let the Games Begin

MJ was busy preening himself, as usual. He was the most arrogant of all of the Deer Folk and had already spent hours combing his hair and polishing his antlers in preparation for the opening parade. He would be leading the gladiators into the arena and wanted to look his best... as always! He was a champion of the games. The previous year he had won seven gold medals and lifted the Lazlo Cup for the ninth year in a row. He had already decided that this year would be number ten.

MJ was eight feet tall, ten if you included his antlers. With his wavy blond hair and piercing green eyes, MJ was a very handsome beast, and didn't he know it! When he trotted past the crowds of spectators, he would wave his head from side to side so that his long hair would flow behind him, glistening in the sunlight.

There were ten games in total, although one was a team sport, the Tug o' War. MJ never took part in that, as he liked to stand out from the crowd, and you can't do that in a Tug o' War.

The Tug o' War is very similar to the human version of the game, with eight 'tuggers' in each team pulling a giant rope in opposite directions. The winning team is the one that manages to pull the other side over the line drawn on the ground between the two teams at the start of the game. The difference is that in the Great Games they really take the war part of the game to heart. Each of the teams has another eight players, known as 'soldiers'. The soldiers fire arrows, cannonballs and boulders at the opposing team as they are pulling. If one of the pullers is hit, then one of the soldiers, or the coach, can replace them. Each team has nine substitutes in total.

Traditionally the first event of the Great Games, the Tug o' War always starts when the sun begins to set. Eight teams compete in the first round. The four winning teams compete in the second round, and the two winning teams then face each other in the final. The final is extremely dangerous for participants, as to add to the excitement the audience are given bags of darts to throw at the teams as they compete. The Tug o' War has a lot of casualties, which is another reason why MJ never competed in it. He would not want to be hit on his beautiful face by a boulder, or by any other flying object lobbed into the arena.

A loud hail of bagpipes and trumpets sounded for the competitors to assemble at the entrance to the arena. MJ proudly took his place in the centre at the front. The reigning champion always leads the other competitors into the arena, with each group holding their herd's flag out in front.

The Lochranza flag was purple with four squares. In three of the squares there was a picture. Top left, a castle; top right, a dragon's head; bottom left, an arrow. Bottom

The Lochranza flag

right was blank, to represent the invisible hypnotic gas that protects the castle.

MJ entered the arena with his head held high, and the flag slightly off to the side. He didn't want the flag to block anyone's view of him. Immediately behind him were the Deer Folk of Lochranza, including one female competitor called Serena. MJ did not like Serena one bit. Not only was she a fantastic gladiator, but she was also very beautiful with violet hair down to her waist and big wide eyes to match. MJ did not like anyone who was better looking than him.

There were twenty-five competitors from Lochranza. Behind them were the Deer Folk from Skye, Islay, Muck,

Eigg, Rum, Canna and Tiree. In total, there were two hundred gladiators competing for the Lazlo Cup.

The gladiators bowed towards the royal box as they entered the arena behind MJ. King Rohan was standing in the box with Queen Sofia by his side. The King and Queen clapped each gladiator as they passed. King Rohan was very tall and handsome, with a chisel jaw and dark hair which had patches of grey dotted randomly through it. Sofia was younger than Rohan. She had white hair and pale pink eyes. You could tell she was a gentle soul with a kind heart just from looking at her.

After circling the entire arena twice, MJ led the majority of the competitors to the sidelines. The Tug o' War teams headed to the centre of the arena. First up was Islay versus Eigg. The tug was over in ten seconds flat with Islay the resounding winners.

The crowd erupted in an equal chorus of cheers and boos at the result, but no one could have been surprised, as the Deer Folk from Eigg are only a few feet tall, whereas the Deer Folk from Islay, known as the 'big yins', are the tallest species of all Deer Folk.

The two teams to reach the final were Muck and Rum. Funnily enough, the members of these teams resembled their own island's name: the Deer Folk from Muck were absolutely filthy and the team from Rum were all very tipsy from drinking large jugs of rum between every game.

The games master shouted out "Tug!" and they started to pull on their respective sides of the rope. Within a few seconds, three of the pullers on the Muck side had fallen. They had all been battered by the same huge boulder. Then, another two fell after being hit by darts from a group of older school kids standing in the front row of spectators. Five soldiers went on as substitutes, but no sooner had they put their hands on the rope than down came another hail of darts from the row of kids. All five substitutes hit the deck.

Bruiser, the Muck team coach started yelling from sidelines, "Get a grip, yah bunch of Jessies."

Bruiser was an enormous creature, easily fourteen feet tall with his huge antlers. His arms were as thick as tree trunks and he had a beard all the way down to his waist. Bruiser had decided it was time to step in! He took hold of the rope, and with one tug the entire Rum team went flying into the air and fell on the other side of the line. They were all hiccupping as they landed, one on top of the other, in a huge heap, their hooves and antlers sticking out all over the place.

"And the winners are… Muck," hollered the games master as he walked over to Bruiser to hold his hand up in victory. But Bruiser was so tall that the games master could only manage to raise his arm to shoulder level. Even though it was more of a hand straight out in the victory punch, there was a huge roar and clapping all around the arena for about twenty seconds, then complete silence fell again.

"Thank goodness that's over," grunted MJ. "Now we can get on to the more important events… the ones I'm in."

He strutted over to the archery area, where there was a row of very pretty cheerers, each holding a large wooden bow in one hand and in the other, a quiver containing five long silver arrows. The cheerers passed the bows to the competitors and started to dance, kicking their front legs up high in the air and spinning around, shaking their brightly coloured pom-poms as they spun. Then they shook their short tails towards the spectators. They repeated this display several times, singing as they danced, "Arrows go swift, do not drift, you have to be bold, if you plan to take gold."

The archers took their places. First up was MJ, of course. There was not so much as a whisper around the arena as he took aim. His silver arrow flew towards the target two hundred metres away and hit dead centre.

Next up was Mac from Tiree. He was about the same height and build as MJ, but he had short red frizzy hair with a beard to match. He took aim and again hit the target dead centre.

In this game of archery, each archer has five arrows and must hit the target dead centre every time, but the target gets fifty metres further away with every shot.

By the time they got to the second last arrow, the target was three hundred and fifty metres away and only four of the initial thirty gladiators were left in the game: MJ, Mac, Serena and Geeza. Geeza was a bit of a ducker and a diver from the Isle of Lewis. Lewis wasn't even competing in the games this year, but, Geeza had managed to acquire himself a place by using his great, great, great grandfather as his connection to the Isle of Canna. He had entered as a gladiator for Canna, which caused some booing from those who thought that effectively he was cheating!

MJ hit the target dead centre with his fourth arrow. The arena erupted. There were tears mixed with cheers from those females who just couldn't take the excitement of seeing their handsome hero striding around the arena on a mini victory parade. But the competition was still far from over. Mac now took aim, drawing his bow all the way back and then releasing his silver arrow to fly like a bolt of lightning towards the target. It landed a few metres short. The spectators clapped his gallant effort and Mac bowed his head to thank them for their support before joining the other archers who were out of the competition.

Serena was next to take aim. She gently pulled back on the bow. So gently, that it looked as though the arrow would barely make it out of the bow, let alone all the way to the target. Even so, the arrow glided through the air and hit the target right in the middle of the bull's-eye.

Up stepped Geeza and the cheering which had erupted for Serena was promptly replaced by booing, but the crowd fell silent as Geeza pulled his great bow back. The arrow went hurtling through the air at the speed of light and hit the target just off-centre.

Geeza was out. The crowd did not boo. Instead, they clapped and Geeza bowed his head in thanks as he walked off.

It was now the last arrow each and the target was placed four hundred metres away. MJ took aim, let the last silver arrow go, and bang, it hit the target right in the centre. He turned and grinned at Serena, then murmured, "Beat that if you can."

As Serena moved to the marker and took aim, MJ muttered under his breath, so that only she could hear, "Make sure you don't break a nail." Serena didn't even turn to look at him. She focused on the target. Then, just as before, she gently pulled back on her bow. The arrow flew gracefully through the air as if floating on an invisible cushion, but instead of aiming for her own target, the arrow was heading for MJ's. Next thing, the crowd started stamping their hooves and shouting, "Winner! Winner!

Winner!" Serena's arrow had split straight through MJ's arrow, breaking it in two. It fell to the ground.

Only one arrow now remained in the target, and that was Serena's.

MJ took the bow off his back and threw it to the ground. When the spectators clapped him, instead of bowing his head in thanks as his predecessors had done, he turned and trotted off into the changing rooms under the stadium without so much as congratulating Serena.

Serena, however, gracefully bowed her head to the cheering spectators, then again to receive her gold medal from the games master. There are no silver or bronze medals awarded at the games. There is only one winner per game and they receive the gold medal. The gladiator with the most gold medals at the end of the games wins the Lazlo Cup. For the Tug o' War a separate medal awarded to the coach of the winning team could be passed to the best member of the team, which would count as one gold medal for that gladiator.

The score after the first two games was zero medals for MJ!

Chapter 7

The Secret of the Ollpheist

When the creature was sure Rhino had gone, it flew back down towards Lochranza Castle and landed gently beside the huge iron gates. It lowered its head to allow Thumble Tumble to slide off onto the grass. The creature's huge head then rose back up and started to shake side to side. Large chunks of seaweed flew off, landing all around Thumble Tumble's feet. The creature was roaring so loudly that Thumble Tumble thought it was in pain, before she realised it sounded more like laughter. She looked up, expecting to see twenty peering spider's eyes and a set of poisonous pincers. But instead, there was a dragon with a huge smile laughing down at her. With seaweed now scattered all over the grass and parts of the castle wall and gates, Thumble Tumble could see that the Ollpheist wasn't a four-headed scary monster. It was a giant purple dragon with round green eyes and a green tip at the end of its long purple tail.

"That was such a laugh," said the dragon.

Thumble Tumble took a step back in shock. She didn't

know dragons could speak.

The dragon leaned down and wrapped his wing round her back, causing Thumble Tumble to jump with fright. But the dragon just kept smiling at her and she realised he was only trying to stop her from tripping over the clumps of slippery seaweed lying on the ground.

"Who are you?" she asked, still trembling.

"Please don't be afraid. My name is Jock. I am the last of the Sea Dragons."

Thumble Tumble had never heard of a Sea Dragon before.

Without thinking she blurted out, "And what makes a Sea Dragon different from an ordinary dragon?" Immediately she realised how rude she must sound. "I'm so sorry. What I meant to ask is, what is exactly is a Sea Dragon?"

"Well," said Jock, "instead of breathing out fire, we Sea Dragons breathe out water – lots of water. During the great battle, when the coven was broken, we helped the good witches fight evil. The water we breathe out is so pure it can actually melt a dark witch if she is blasted with it for long enough. Usually thirty seconds does the trick, but for a particularly evil witch it can take twice as long."

Wow, thought Thumble Tumble.

"It must be amazing to have the power to melt a dark witch," she said.

Jock suddenly looked as though he was about to burst into tears.

"It is pretty cool," he agreed. "But also sad, because every Sea Dragon on Earth was destroyed by the dark witches. All except me. When they found out about our special powers, Mogdred, the supreme dark witch, ordered the destruction of all Sea Dragons. It was just over ten years ago when the last of the Sea Dragons were slain. They were my parents. I was still an egg and just before the dark witches came, my mother hid me in a pool. The only person who knew of my existence was a three-legged Haggis called McCools. He dropped me into the bottom of Domhain Loch to save me."

Thumble Tumble had a lump in her throat. She too had lost her parents when she was very young. So young, in fact, that she couldn't remember them at all.

"How did you manage to survive?" she asked Jock.

"I almost didn't," Jock told her. When I hatched I was so small I didn't know what to do, so I swam straight to the surface. Luckily, I was spotted there by King Rohan and Queen Sofia. If it hadn't been for them, I would never have survived. They gave me food and shelter. They also started the rumour of the Ollpheist, the terrible four-headed monster that lives at the bottom of Domhain Loch. They made up the story of the monster to stop anyone from coming near the loch. They even told people about Deer Folk going into the loch looking for the monster and disappearing! Before long the rumours became accepted as reality and I became a legend, the legend of the Ollpheist."

Thumble Tumble thought how lucky she was to have her aunts, even if her parents were gone. She couldn't begin to imagine how lonely it must have been for Jock with no family, all alone at the bottom of the loch.

"I have had to hide in the loch my entire life," Jock continued. "If any dark witches find out that there is still a Sea Dragon alive, they will hunt me down and kill me. It's pretty lonely being the last Sea Dragon on Earth," he

Thumble Tumble dips her feet into Domhain Loch

added mournfully, staring deep into the loch.

Jock waded into the loch and rested his head on the shore. Thumble Tumble sat down beside him, looked into his big green eyes, and started to tell him all about Auntie Bessie's wacky spells and Auntie Isla's famous Scoffalicious Chocolate which she was delivering to King Rohan so that she could sneak into the Great Games. She took off her pink Converse trainers and dipped her feet in the water as they spoke, even though she was still wearing her stripy tights! The cold water sent a tingling feeling up through her legs that felt fab. Thumble Tumble had wanted to put her feet in Domhain Loch for a long time, but she had been afraid to do it in case her toes were eaten by the Ollpheist!

"Not much chance of that," laughed Jock. "I'm a vegetarian. I mainly eat seaweed… and the occasional giant of course!"

They both burst out laughing. They were having so much fun, they hadn't noticed that the sky above them had turned dark, and that the air had an extra icy chill in it.

Chapter 8

Spoilsports

MJ was still in the changing room, moaning at the fact he'd been beaten by a girl, and a beautiful girl at that.

Could things get any worse? he thought to himself.

Just at that moment, he heard what sounded like a stampede of hooves followed by very loud screaming. Not the kind of screaming he was used to, the sound of girls screaming fanatically, but actual screams of fear.

MJ bolted back up to the arena. There were Deer Folk running in all directions. The competitors were sprinting towards the stands, away from the arena, whilst the spectators were running into the arena, away from the stands. They were crashing into each other, their antlers getting tangled and stuck, making them fall to the ground. In the midst of the chaos, MJ heard a whooshing sound and his left ear felt as though it had been grazed by fire. Next, there was a crashing sound beside his left hoof. He looked down to see the ground cracked open where a thunderbolt had struck, leaving a circle of black powder to mark the spot. When he looked up to the sky, he knew instantly they were under attack from Night Witches.

MJ hardly had time to wonder how they had got past the tower guards when dozens more thunderbolts came raining down from the black skies above. Everyone was going to have to take cover. As MJ headed towards the centre of the arena, the hail of thunderbolts followed him. He deliberately flicked his long blond hair to attract attention, hoping to draw their aim away from the panicked crowds. Sure enough, even more thunderbolts headed his way.

"Get the school kids and take cover in the changing rooms," he shouted to the cheerers.

They immediately followed his instructions. After all, MJ was King Rohan's son, Prince of Lochranza!

Extremely agile, MJ started weaving swiftly from side to side, dodging the thunderbolts as he led them further away from the spectators.

Although he was arrogant, MJ was also very brave and would do anything to protect his people from harm.

"Where are my parents?" he called to the royal guards. Before they could answer, he spotted the King and Queen leading fleeing spectators into the castle. King Rohan was fighting off Night Witches alongside his guards and Queen Sofia was helping to carry the injured inside.

MJ was soon joined in the arena by Mac and Geeza. They both had their bows in hand and their quivers loaded with arrows. Geeza was carrying a spare bow, which he threw over to MJ. From out of nowhere, Serena appeared with his quiver, also jammed full of arrows.

The four gladiators started to shoot huge silver arrows into the air towards the Night Witches, who were circling so fast and so high, it was difficult to hit them. They were

MJ, Prince of the Deer Folk

also difficult to spot, as they stayed within the dark clouds, making them virtually invisible.

Mac took aim and hit the back of a broom. The broom started spinning out of control and threw the witch off, far into the Giant Hills. Then MJ managed to shoot straight through one of the Night Witch's brooms. But as the witch was falling to the ground, another zoomed in and grabbed her, and the pair flew off back into the clouds, cackling as they soared.

Mac hit another Night Witch, then Geeza got one, then MJ. Four witches were now spinning out of control on their brooms. Surprisingly, Serena hadn't managed to hit a single Night Witch, after being such an excellent shot in the archery competition. The four gladiators formed a square, facing out, in the centre of the arena, firing their arrows miles up into the darkness. The Night Witches came back at them in force, firing thunderbolts from all directions, fast and furious.

They formed a circle above the gladiators' heads and started swooping towards them in pairs, firing lightning bolts with every swoop. Mac fell to the ground, hit on the shoulder, his blood pouring onto the arena floor.

"Cover Mac," MJ called to Serena.

As he turned to fire his next arrow, a bolt went hurtling past his head towards his injured friend. MJ tried to grab the bolt with his hand, but it passed straight through his fingers, singing the tips before striking Mac on his leg just above the knee. The Night Witches had now completely surrounded them, and they were closing in.

It was only a matter of time before the four gladiators ran out of arrows.

Realising that Mac urgently needed help soon, or he might die, MJ grabbed his good arm. "You'll have to run on three legs, can you manage it?" he asked urgently.

Mac nodded.

"OK, on the count of three we go. One… two… " but before MJ could say three, another lightning bolt crashed down and sent him, Geeza and Serena hurtling to the ground.

MJ jumped back up as quick as a flash and grabbed three arrows from his bow. He fired the arrows simultaneously at the three Night Witches who were heading towards them. Each was holding a Death Bolt, aimed straight at the fallen gladiators. MJ hit all three of the witches who shrieked and wailed as they fell to the ground. He was still loading his bow when two more witches appeared.

"Get him out of here," MJ shouted to Serena and Geeza, pointing at Mac. But instead, Serena took an arrow from her quiver and stabbed Geeza in the back with it. Geeza fell beside Mac, his body completely still, his eyes wide open, staring up into the dark skies above.

MJ couldn't believe the evidence of his own eyes. Serena, helping the Night Witches! Now two of his friends lying dead or dying!

Like a raging bull, he charged at the oncoming Night Witches, his head bowed low and his piercing antlers out in front of him.

Serena lifted her bow and took aim.

Chapter 9

Melting Pot

Thumble Tumble suddenly had a feeling of dread come over her. She had felt this type of cold before, a long time ago. This was nothing like a normal rush of cold air. The air was cutting into her bones. It felt like someone was poking ice-cold needles into her skin. And the darkness was not the usual dark of night. It was as though someone had lifted a giant blanket and placed it over the sky. There was not a sliver of light to be seen. No stars or moons in the distance, just a huge black cloud that went on forever.

Then, almost as quickly as it had arrived, the chilling darkness started to disappear. The air got slightly warmer, and Thumble Tumble could feel the tips of her fingers again. They were tingling as though she had just plunged them into boiling hot water. When she looked up, she saw shafts of light starting to cut through the black clouds.

"Thank goodness they've gone. I think that was the Night Witches, Jock. They must have seen you, or that horrible giant told them about you."

Jock, still looking up at the sky, replied, "I don't think

A cyclone of witches above Lochranza Castle

they're looking for me."

Thumble Tumble looked back up. The most gigantic cyclone of black and grey clouds was forming right above Lochranza Castle. In amongst the clouds, she could see the vague outline of what looked like witches on brooms, flying into the cyclone towards the castle.

"Come on, we have to help them," cried Thumble Tumble. She sprang to her feet and started running towards her broom.

Jock didn't move a muscle. He was frozen to the spot.

"I'm sorry Thumble Tumble," he said in a trembling voice. "I can't come with you. If they see me, they'll know there's still a living Sea Dragon and they'll hunt me down until I'm dead."

Thumble Tumble could see the fear in Jock's eyes. She didn't want to put him in danger, so without uttering another word she got onto her broom and headed for the castle.

Thumble Tumble flew straight into Lochranza Castle. Not a single arrow was fired to stop her. There didn't seem to be any Deer Folk guarding the perimeter from the turrets.

That's very strange, she thought uneasily. She glanced back to see what had happened to the guards in the turrets – and crashed straight into a broom which was unmanned because the Night Witch who had been flying it had been evaporated by one of MJ's arrows. Thumble Tumble came hurtling off her broom, but luckily she wasn't very high off the ground and didn't have far to fall. Also, her landing was broken, as she fell straight into the lap of a female Deer Folk whose violet hair was now twisted around Thumble Tumble's waist.

"I'm so sorry," stuttered Thumble Tumble trying to disentangle herself from the long strands of hair.

"Don't make another move!" commanded MJ.

He was standing over Thumble Tumble with a huge silver arrow aimed straight at her chest.

Thumble Tumble started to shake from head to toe, until it dawned on her that the arrow wasn't pointed at her chest but at Serena's hand, which grasped a dagger poised to stab her in the heart.

At MJ's warning, Serena dropped the dagger.

"Who are you?" MJ asked Thumble Tumble, as he tied Serena's hands behind her back.

As MJ pulled the ropes more tightly around her wrists, Serena glared at Thumble Tumble.

"I'm Thumble Tumble. I was supposed to be delivering Scoffalicious Chocolate to King Rohan for my Auntie Isla," Thumble Tumble replied.

MJ took a long look at Thumble Tumble.

"So, you're Lizzie's daughter. We'd better get you out of here, pronto! But first, can you help me with these two?" he nodded over to Mac and Geeza.

"No problem," replied Thumble Tumble.

She helped Mac back up onto his hooves and placed her broom under his arm like a crutch.

MJ was still bending over Geeza's apparently lifeless body, when without warning Geeza sat bolt upright with his bow in his hand, and fired. The shot took out a hideous Night Witch who was flying directly towards them.

"You guys run. I'll give you cover," Geeza urged, pulling another arrow from his quiver.

"I'm not leaving you," MJ insisted.

"MJ, I won't make it. The wound is too deep," Geeza said.

"Please try, Geeza," pleaded MJ.

"I can't stand up. Please… you need to save the others," replied Geeza.

MJ turned round just in time to see another dozen Night Witches swooping towards them in a Death Circle. There were no arrows left in his quiver. He took his bow and swung it around his head, then let go. The bow whirled past all twelve witches, knocking them to the ground one at a time. It then came back round like a boomerang straight into MJ's hand. He caught hold, but a lightning bolt hit his hand, blasting the bow straight back out of it to land on the ground twenty feet away.

Night Witches were circling above their heads faster

and faster, cackling with glee. Each pointed a long black finger towards their target and started to chant a death bolt spell, then… *blast!* Before the death bolts could be summoned, a huge jet of water blasted the circle of witches apart and their brooms completely disintegrated under the impact.

The Night Witches started to fizzle and fry as soon as the water touched them, then they started to melt, black smoke bellowing from their cloaks. The smoke was so thick that MJ and Thumble Tumble could see nothing.

Jock flew towards them.

"Get out of here!" he shouted, before flying back up into the air to fire another huge jet of water into the circle of Night Witches.

Thumble Tumble grabbed Geeza under his arms and started dragging him across the arena towards the castle. Mac hobbled alongside them, using her broom as a crutch. They could hear the Night Witches flying back up into the black cyclone in which they had arrived, screeching at the top of their lungs, "Sea Dragon! Retreat!"

When the smoke finally cleared, all that remained of the Night Witches were a few charred cloaks lying like puddles of mud on the ground, and some grey ash where their brooms had disintegrated. There was no sign of Serena, and no one could begin to understand why she had helped the Night Witches attack them.

Chapter 10

Snatched

Serena slowly opened her eyes. The room was in complete darkness, the ice cold air thick with the stench of rotten cabbages.

The putrid smell almost made her vomit. Serena put her hands out and touched what she thought must be a wall. It was cold and slimy, with some kind of gooey liquid dripping down onto the floor below. She felt her way around the walls. There were no doors or windows, and not a solitary ray of light anywhere.

She couldn't quite remember how she had got there, but she knew exactly where she was – Mogdred's dungeon!

Serena would never forget the last time she had been a 'guest' in Mogdred's dungeon, almost a year ago. That was the last time she had seen her sister Alfy.

Alfy had been playing at the edge of the Light and Dark Forest, near the swamps, when Ugg and Ogg spotted her. She was chasing Snozel Frazens – tiny insects that fly up your nose and make you sneeze. The Snozel Frazens were tickling the inside of her nose then flying out just before she sneezed.

Their hive was suspended above a sinking swamp, on the branch of an old oak tree. Alfy was having so much fun, she had failed to see the swamp. The tears of laughter that were streaming down her face turned to tears of fear when she realised she was sinking into the swamp.

Alfy struggled furiously, but the more she struggled the deeper she sank.

"Help! Help me!" she screamed at the top of her lungs.

In their hundreds, the little Snozel Frazens tried to pull her free, but despite their numbers they were too small.

One of them flew off as fast as it could to get help. Serena was tracking Alfy's hoof prints when the Snozel Frazen flew straight into her eye.

"Watch out!" she yelped, flicking the insect out of her lashes.

The Snozel Frazen flew frantically back and forth between the ground where Alfy's hoof print was and the direction of the swamp.

"What's wrong?" cried Serena, suddenly alarmed. "Is it Alfy? Show me!"

The tiny insect zoomed through the trees towards the swamp with Serena galloping close behind.

When they arrived, there was no sign of Alfy.

Serena began weeping. "No! No!" she wailed up into the trees.

The Snozel Frazens were flying around her head, banging into her cheeks, and hovering in her ears. They seemed to be humming "Alfy".

"Leave me alone!" Serena shouted, brushing the clouds of Snozel Frazens away with her hands.

Then she noticed that the insects had swarmed into the

A Snozel Frazen

shape of an arrow that pointed at the edge of the swamp.

"Troll prints!" Serena said aloud. "Do Tree Trolls have my sister?" she gasped.

"Yes they do," hummed the Snozel Frazens.

Serena tracked the Tree Trolls through the Light and Dark Forest into the Forbidden Valley, travelling day and night without rest. After three days of searching, she finally caught up with her sister's captors.

They had set up camp in a cave at the very bottom of the valley. Serena slipped into the cave without making a sound. Ugg and Ogg were boasting to one another about how they had saved Alfy from the sinking swamp.

"I thank you for that," said Serena, now standing right above the two Tree Trolls, who were sitting on the ground tucking into a feast of bugs. "But what I don't understand is why or where you then took her?"

"Oh, that would be because I told them to bring her to me," came an eerie whisper from the back of the cave.

A severe chill spiked through the air and a foul smell started wafting towards Serena.

"What do you want with my sister?" Serena asked the creature lurking in the darkness.

"Nothing," replied Mogdred. "It's you I need!"

Serena began edging her way back towards the cave entrance, only to discover it was gone!

"Welcome to my lair," hissed Mogdred. "As they say, one good turn deserves another," she continued. "I saved your sister, and now

I want you to do something in return for me."

"And if I don't want to do something?" Serena said grimly.

"Then I'm afraid your sister will have to remain my 'guest'… forever!" said Mogdred turning back towards the rear of the dungeon.

"What exactly do you want me to do?" asked Serena reluctantly.

"There are some ROYAL PESTS I need to get rid of," screeched Mogdred. "When you have done this small deed for me, I will return your sister."

"How do I know you'll keep your word?" demanded Serena.

"You don't," cackled Mogdred. Then she flicked her long black finger at Serena.

The next thing Serena remembered was waking up at the edge of the Light and Dark Forest, all alone, without Alfy!

Chapter 11

Lazlo's Cup

Thumble Tumble let go of Geeza's arm as soon as they entered the great hall inside the castle. Right away, two of the cheerers were by his side. One had a long sharp needle with steel thread and the other had her arms full of bandages. They set to work straight away stitching up the huge gash in Geeza's back, before wrapping him up in so many bandages he looked like a mummy.

Mac was being looked after by two equally beautiful cheerers, who were tending to his leg and shoulder wounds.

"Here you go, miss," he said to Thumble Tumble, handing her broom back. "We are forever in your debt. If you and your friend hadn't arrived when you did, the Night Witches would have killed us for sure."

Mac had a deep voice that for some reason sounded familiar to Thumble Tumble.

She felt as though she must have met him before. In fact, she was sure she had met all of them before – Mac, MJ and Geeza.

"This is Lizzie's daughter," MJ announced.

"I might have known," sighed Mac. "No ordinary girl would try to take on a group of Night Witches armed with just a broom!"

"Did you know my mother?" asked Thumble Tumble.

"That we did, young lady. A finer witch I've never met. We fought together to protect the coven from the Night Witches. She put her life on the line many times to save others." Mac was just about to launch into a long reminiscence when King Rohan entered the hall.

"I think that's enough chat about the past," said the King, glaring towards Mac.

" I'd really like to know more about my mother. I didn't even know she had fought against the Night Witches," murmured Thumble Tumble.

"I'm afraid that's a conversation for another day," said the King. "We still have eight magnificent games to watch and I was wondering if you and Jock would care to join us in the royal box?"

"Would we ever!" chorused Thumble Tumble and Jock excitedly. They followed the King through the great hall to a narrow staircase that spiralled up to the top level of the castle walls.

Jock was determined not to miss out on this fantastic opportunity. He took a deep breath, pulled his tummy in as far as he could, then squeezed himself up the stairs to an opening at the top that was no bigger than a standard door entrance.

When he finally squashed through he found himself in the royal box. It was enormous, which was certainly not what he'd expected as he'd squeezed his huge body the whole way up the stairs. There were no seats in the royal box, just a small bench along the viewing deck. It was very plush, with gold legs and cushions covered in a deep purple velvety material. This was not for sitting on. It was so that the King and Queen could kneel down on their front legs if they got tired.

Queen Sofia was already in the box when they entered along with two royal guards and a strange looking little man with a big red whistle and lots of bits of paper. Thumble Tumble bowed as soon as she saw the Queen and Jock bent over as much as he could. Not quite a bow, but as close as he could get to one with his huge stomach.

"Please stand up," said the Queen in a soft comforting voice. "This is our games master, Mr Pimbleton," she said, pointing to the strange little man standing beside her.

"Pleased to meet you," said Thumble Tumble courteously, and shook Mr Pimbleton's hand.

"Very pleased to meet you too," gabbled Mr Pimbleton as he frantically shook Thumble Tumble's hand.

"Well I'd better get back to the arena," he said hurriedly. He bowed to the Queen, nodded at Thumble Tumble and Jock, and rushed out of the royal box. No sooner had he disappeared through the doorway when he re-appeared right in the middle of the arena below, blowing his big red whistle.

Jock and Thumble Tumble glanced at one another in disbelief.

The gladiators were back on the field and the spectators were in their viewing boxes. The cheerers had cleared up the remains of the Night Witches and the entire arena was now lit by the giant burning torches that were lined up along the top of the castle walls.

There were three gladiators missing from the games:

Serena, Geeza and MJ. MJ had decided not to participate further, and instead joined his young guests alongside his parents in the royal box.

Geeza was still recovering in the hospital wing of the castle, and Serena had fled!

Mac was now bandaged up and back in the arena with his two beautiful cheerers looking after him.

The next game was 'Throwing the Boulder'. Each contestant has to select a boulder and throw it as far as they can. The winner is the one who throws the heaviest boulder the furthest. The catch is that the gladiators are blindfolded and have to use their instincts so as not to throw any boulders at the spectators. In the past many spectators had ended up with boulders crashing onto them.

"That is why the royal box is so high up," laughed Queen Sofia.

The competition was soon well under way. Two gladiators from Rum had thrown their boulders straight into the spectators on the south side of the arena, actually injuring more Deer Folk with their poor aim than the Night Witches had managed to do during their attack!

There were now five gladiators left to throw.

Just as the next gladiator lifted his massive boulder above his head, two witches came flying into the arena in a veil of purple smoke. The guards in the royal box drew their bows to fire into the ball of smoke.

"Stillamomentum!" hollered one of the witches, raising her wand towards the sky.

Everyone stood motionless as the two witches flew into the royal box and dismounted from their brooms. Within a few seconds the effects of the pausing spell wore off. The poor gladiator who had been holding the massive boulder

The Lazlo Cup

above his head couldn't hold the weight any longer, and it dropped onto his two front hooves.

"We are so sorry to interrupt your majesties, but we were extremely worried about Thumble Tumble," said Isla, glaring at Thumble Tumble. "We told her to be home before dark!"

"Please don't be angry, Isla," said Queen Sofia. "If it wasn't for Thumble Tumble, tonight we would have lost some of our finest gladiators to the Night Witches."

Queen Sofia told Isla and Bessie about the day's events, and how brave Thumble Tumble had been in the battle against the Night Witches.

Thumble Tumble was surprised by how well her aunts seemed to know the Queen. They spoke together as though they were old friends, although she had never heard them mention Queen Sofia before.

Queen Sofia invited Isla and Bessie to join them for the remainder of the games and three of them chatted quietly at the back of the royal box. Thumble Tumble tried to overhear what they were talking about, but the cheers from the spectators were too loud and she was enjoying the games so much she soon forgot that they were there.

It was past midnight when the last game finished and the champion of the gladiators was announced. Mr Pimbleton was standing in the centre of the arena with a little rusty cup. He had swapped his red whistle for a bright yellow megaphone, which he was now tapping frantically to test the volume.

"Ladies and Gentlemen, with a total of six medals the winner of the Lazlo Cup this year is… Mac of Tiree."

There was a huge uproar around the arena and the spectators started clapping and stamping their hooves in celebration.

The rusty little cup didn't look very grand. In fact, it didn't look at all like the proper cup for such a prestigious competition. Looks, however, can be deceiving. This little cup held a great power – the power to melt a frozen heart. The cup had been enchanted thousands of years earlier by a powerful wizard called Lazlo. He had fallen in love with a beautiful princess, Jacqueline Frost (sister of Jack). But her heart was made of ice so cold that she couldn't love him back. Lazlo was so distraught he travelled to the Earth's core and forged a cup out of molten iron ore. He then cast a magical spell that transfers the power of the smouldering heat into the person drinking from the cup. When Jacqueline drank from the cup, her ice-cold heart melted and she was able to fall in love with Lazlo. She could never go back to the icy cold land where she had lived with her brother. So from that day on, it was only 'Jack Frost' who would go out to play on a frosty day.

The story of Lazlo and Jacqueline made the gladiators believe that the cup had the power to make someone fall in love with them. The fought fiercely each year to win the cup and gain true love. It was only after winning it that they would find out that it did not have the power to make someone fall in love, only the power to melt an ice-cold heart!

Mac walked over to the winner's podium, but instead of taking the cup he whispered something into Mr Pimbleton's ear. A second later, Mr Pimbleton had disappeared from the arena and was now standing right beside Thumble Tumble in the royal box.

"I'm afraid we need you at the podium, my dear." As he spoke he took hold of Thumble Tumble's hand and in the blink of an eye she was standing beside Mac on the winner's podium.

Mr Pimbleton picked up his bright yellow megaphone and announced through it, "Ladies and Gentlemen, in a surprise turn of events the winner of the Lazlo Cup this year is Thumble Tumble. The Lazlo Cup has been passed to her by Mac for her bravery and excellent battle skills. But mainly for saving his life!"

Mr Pimbleton had a little chuckle, then he handed Thumble Tumble the rusty cup and shook her hand so much she thought her arm was going to pop out of its socket.

Thumble Tumble held the cup high in the air and the whole arena erupted in loud cheering. She had thought the games would be awesome, but they were way better than she had imagined. She just couldn't picture the day getting any better – at least, not until Auntie Isla announced that the Scoffalicious Chocolate was now ready to eat.

Thumble Tumble rushed back up to the royal box, where she and Jock took a huge chunk of chocolate, respectively savouring the delicious flavours of Chocolate Strawberries and Luminous Seaweed as they sat back and watched the cheerers performing their dances well into the wee hours.

Chapter 12

Return of the Protector

By the time Thumble Tumble woke up the next day the sun was already high in the sky. She was so exhausted from partying at the Great Games that she had slept straight through the 'Podi Alarm' and breakfast! As she sleepily made her way downstairs she could hear her aunts chatting in hushed, somewhat frantic tones.

"Morning!" she said cheerily as she entered the kitchen.

"Oh, good morning," replied Isla, sounding rather odd. "We didn't hear you come down."

Isla then turned her back on Thumble Tumble and started putting random ingredients into a cauldron that was bubbling on the stove.

Bessie was also acting out of character. The second Thumble Tumble walked through the kitchen door, she had stopped talking. And Auntie Bessie rarely, if ever, stopped talking – let alone in mid-sentence!

"Is everything OK?" asked Thumble Tumble. "You two are acting really strangely!"

Isla and Bessie looked at one another solemnly, then

The little white cottage where Thumble Tumble lives

Bessie took a deep breath.

"We think it's time for you to develop your Protective Virtuosities."

"My Protective Virtosisis?" replied Thumble Tumble, sounding confused.

"Oh, for goodness sake, Bessie, she's eight, not eighty!

Isla then addressed Thumble Tumble.

 "She means your Pro V's."

"Woohoo!" cheered Thumble Tumble, throwing her arms in the air. She burst into a celebratory jog around the kitchen.

"All right, that's enough hilarity," Bessie said sternly. "Your Protective Virtuosities are very important, and if you cannot take them seriously then obviously we were mistaken and you are not ready yet!"

"No, no – I am ready. Honestly, I just got a bit excited. I mean the Great Games *and* my Pro V's in the same week – you'd be excited too!"

"OK," nodded Bessie in agreement. "Now quickly conjure yourself up some toast and meet us in the back garden." Bessie snapped her fingers and disappeared.

Thumble Tumble took her wand out from a fold in her pyjamas and pointed it towards a slice of bread that was lying on a plate beside the toaster.

"She didn't mean literally," laughed Isla as she lifted the slice of bread and dropped it into the toaster.

She winked at Thumble Tumble and left the kitchen the same way Bessie had.

When Thumble Tumble arrived in the back garden there were six crooked witches' hats lined up on top of the fence.

The garden was spread over three levels. On the top level grew beds of brightly coloured herbs and spices, each one having a magical component.

A narrow set of stairs led to the middle level, which resembled a patio, but instead of paving stones the ground was covered with dozens of lily pads gently floating in an inch of water. The patio was adorned with a big oak table and three chairs.

The stairs continued down to the bottom level. This looked more like woodland than someone's garden. It was lined on either side by ancient yew trees with a stream meandering along the bottom.

Just in front of the stream there was a small fence, which was currently home to the hats of six deceased Night Witches.

Thumble Tumble rushed down towards the bottom level with her wand eagerly poised.

"The first Protective Virtuosity is how to disarm your opponent," bellowed Bessie, as though she was addressing an entire classroom of schoolchildren. "You must take aim." Then she shouted out "Neutraleosis!" and with that an orange light shot out of the tip of her wand.

The light beam struck the first hat, which instantly combusted.

"You try now," she said turning to Thumble Tumble, feeling very pleased with herself.

Thumble Tumble took out her wand and pointed it in the direction of the fence. Her hand was shaking as she blurted out the spell: "Neutral-o-sis!"

A puff of orange smoke emerged from the tip of her wand and landed in a heap at her feet.

"Not to worry," Isla interjected. "That's happened to me loads! The spell is pronounced 'Neutral-e-o-sis'. Let's try again."

Thumble Tumble carefully aimed her wand at the second hat perched on the fence and then in a very deliberate voice said, "Neutral-e-o-sis!"

This time, a beam of orange light came spurting out of her wand. It shot straight over the fence, just missing a squirrel before blasting into an elm tree on the far side of the stream.

"That was *much* better," said Isla encouragingly. "This time, try not to close your eyes when you fire the light bolt."

Thumble Tumble nodded as she took aim for a third time.

"Neutraleosis!" she yelled, keeping her eyes firmly on the target.

The beam of orange light swooped straight towards the second hat, knocking it clean off the fence.

"Well done," hollered Isla and Bessie in unison.

Thumble Tumble took a little bow, then spun round to deal with the four remaining hats.

Serena also woke up late that morning. The last thing she could remember about the Great Games was being pulled up into the air, then being hit by a thunderbolt in the stomach. The force of the bolt was so strong that it had knocked her out.

She was still feeling dazed when she heard a horribly familiar voice from the corner of the room.

"You failed me. I held up my part of the bargain. But you couldn't even defeat a child and her pet dragon!"

There was a dull light moving across the room towards her.

Mogdred was pointing her long black finger straight at Serena's head. She hissed as she spoke and her horrible breath made Serena gag.

"The dragon certainly defeated your army," Serena barked back. She was fearless, even with the most evil of all of the Night Witches standing over her about to cast a death spell.

"Don't worry, Serena," said Mogdred in a low, eerie voice. "We will hunt the Sea Dragon down. We killed every other Sea Dragon on the planet so I'm sure we'll manage one more."

Mogdred started chuckling cruelly at the thought of killing Jock, the very last of the Sea Dragons.

She then drew in a deep breath and started to chant a death spell.

She broke off when Serena interrupted her.

"Anyway, it's the child you should be seeking, not the Dragon."

Mogdred ignored her and returned to her chanting.

"Death shall *not* be swift, death *shall* be painful."

Serena felt as if there was a huge invisible hand around her throat squeezing tighter and tighter, choking every last drop of life from her body. She couldn't breathe. She was just about to pass out when she managed to utter seven words which had a dramatic effect on Mogred, who released her spell immediately.

"What did you say?" she shrieked at Serena, who was now rolling around on the floor, gasping for air.

"She has the power of the Protector," Serena repeated in a strained voice.

"How do you know this?"

Mogdred was now standing over Serena, her white eyes wide open.

Serena noticed for the first time that Mogdred had no eyelids.

This must be why she had to stay in the dungeons of her own castle, she thought. *Any light at all must cause her excruciating pain.*

Serena was still staring into the pale eyes when Mogdred grabbed her by her forearms and hauled her up onto her four legs.

"I asked you a question. If you answer correctly, you may just live."

Serena paused for a moment. "She wears the ring. A pink teardrop made from glass."

Many stories of the Protector's powers had been told over the years since Lizzie's death. But the one story that held true was that the power of the Protector had been transferred to a baby via an amulet. That amulet was a pink glass ring, just like the one Serena had seen on Thumble Tumble's little finger.

"Well done, Serena. You live to fight another day… for me."

Mogdred was almost grinning, although it was difficult to see any kind of emotion in her expressionless face.

"We had a deal," snarled Serena through gritted teeth.

"Yes, we did. But you failed, and so now we have another deal: your life in exchange for your services. I am going to need someone to track down this little witch and her dragon so that I can destroy them. Is that agreed, or will I continue my death spell where I left off?"

Serena reluctantly bowed down and once again she felt the piercing pain of a thunderbolt fired into her stomach.

When she lifted her head back up, she found herself standing in front of a little white cottage with a porthole in the centre of the door. She could hear laughter coming from the rear of the cottage, then a very distinct young voice shouted out "Neutraleosis!"

"Gotya!" Serena murmured to herself, and started to slink stealthily along the stone path at the side of the cottage.

Thumble Tumble and the Ollpheist is the first book in a series of eight. Turn the page to read the opening chapter of book two, *Thumble Tumble and the Cauldron of Undry*.

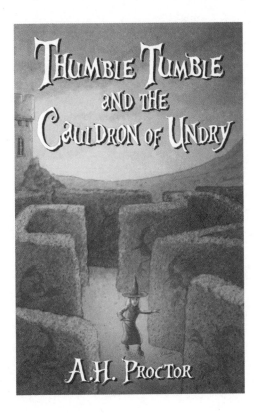

And Then There Was One

Sparkling blue light filled the cave as sunshine reflected off the sapphire crystals that had been lovingly hung from every single stalactite by Morven, the beautiful Sea Dragon who lived there. Her scales shimmered in ever-changing shades of violet and indigo.

It was early evening and Morven was standing over a huge pot in the part of the cave she used as a kitchen because water dripped in from a small hole in the ceiling above. She had once placed the carcass of a little rowing boat under the hole to collect the drips and realised it made the perfect kitchen sink!

Morven was adding various ingredients to the pot, picking them up gently with her teeth and dropping them in. The dish she was so carefully preparing was seaweed stew. A rare treat, because the luminous seaweed needed to make the stew was almost impossible to find, as it only grew in the dark depths of Domhain Loch.

Into the pot went gammell roots. The gammell roots didn't look very appetising. They had thick, black, prickly skin and the smell from them was disgusting. Just like rotting fish!

Morven picked up a few at a time between her teeth and squeezed gently until their pale pink flesh popped out from their skin. As the flesh appeared, she dropped them into the pot. The vegetables tasted nothing like the way they smelled. After shedding their scary looking skin, the pink flesh inside was soft and sweet, with a citrus aroma.

'One for me, one for the pot. One for me, one for the pot,' Morven hummed as she munched her way through half of the huge pile of gammell roots while dropping the other half into the stew.

She started adding spices to season the dish, discussing the merits or otherwise with herself as she went along.

'Mm, a touch more fire chilli I think? Maybe a tad more? Just a snitch more.' She stuck her tongue into the pot… 'Perfect!' she muttered, slurping down a mouthful of stew.

The dragon's home was surprisingly bright and airy, due to a hole in the ceiling near the back of the cave which allowed sunlight to come streaming through.

Despite the brightness, Morven's eyelids felt very heavy. They were drooping halfway down and every now and then she'd find herself standing upright with her eyes completely closed, at which point she would wake up, startled, and give herself a shake. A loud grumbling growl that periodically echoed around the cave walls was also helping to keep her awake. The growls were coming from the bottom of her stomach. Morven had been trawling Domhain Loch all day, looking for luminous seaweed for the stew. And now she was tired and hungry.

Morven and her husband, Tavish, were two of the last remaining Sea Dragons on earth. They had fled to the Isle of Arran, home of Lizzie the Protector, to raise a family. Their first child was still an egg and the precious bundle was due to hatch in just a few weeks. The dark-grey, stripy markings on the shell meant it was a boy.

Morven had been preparing the cave for the new arrival for weeks. She had gathered glistening stones, fluffy wool balls and teething toys made from an array of seashells, rocks and pebbles.

Most importantly, she had been making the baby pool. When they hatch, baby Sea Dragons need to stay submerged in fresh water until all of their scales have fully formed, and this can take up to three months. Morven had dug out a large ditch at the back of the cave to make sure the pool had lots of sunlight. She had lined the pool with clay from the bottom of Domhain Loch and filled it with fresh water from the loch. Everything was ready.

Morven was so excited she couldn't help but smile every time she thought of tiny dragon feet pattering about the cave. But, she was also fearful for her precious little bundle, as she knew that if Mogdred ever found out about the egg, she would do everything in her power to destroy it.

'Tavish should be home any time now,' Morven said aloud to herself.

Gripping with her teeth, she picked up the two massive pieces of slate they used as plates and placed them on the great stone table that stood in the centre of the cave. Next, she took the pot in her mouth and poured huge dollops of seaweed stew onto each of the slates. The luminous seaweed glowed, its yellowish-orange shimmer replacing the blue sparkles, which had mostly disappeared now that the sun had almost set.

Morven had been so preoccupied with making dinner that she got quite a shock when she realised how much the daylight was dimming. As quickly as she could, she began to ignite the dozens of torches set on ledges around the cave, puffing gently on each one until the twine inside burst into flames. Within a few minutes her home was so brightly illuminated you could easily think it was midday and not seven o'clock in the evening. Morven never allowed the cave to fall into complete darkness, especially at night, as that was when the Night Witches were on patrol, looking to attack any unsuspecting victims.

Wondering where on earth Tavish could have got to, Morven decided to eat her helping of stew. An hour passed, then another, and Morven fell asleep. With her mouth wide open, she was snoring so loudly that the sapphire crystals hung all around the cave swayed to and fro, making a soothing, tinkling sound as they chimed against each other. This was the perfect environment for a baby to fall asleep… and its mummy!

In the middle of a lovely dream in which her egg had hatched into a baby Sea dragon, Morven rolled over onto her tummy. As she did so, the tip of her tail hit one of the stalactites growing from the roof of the cave, sending sapphire crystals crashing to the ground. Morven jumped up, startled by the noise and looked around in a sleepy haze.

The first thing she realised was that Tavish still hadn't returned home!

Morven began to get really worried. Tavish always made sure he was home before nightfall, especially since the Night Witch attacks had started.

She went over to the pile of straw neatly packed at the back of the cave and stared adoringly at the fragile little egg that had been placed there. Using her mouth, she carefully transferred it into the baby pool. Once she had made sure that the egg was fully submerged, she gathered twigs and branches in her jaws and placed them in a criss-cross pattern over the pool. When it was completely covered, she took a deep breath and blew dust over the makeshift cover until it blended in with the rest of the floor.

Just then, an enormous gust of wind surged through the cave, extinguishing every one of the torches she had lit earlier and throwing her to the ground.

There was not a single shred of light anywhere. Morven blinked frantically, her large green eyes trying to adjust to the pitch black.

Then, she heard Tavish crying out to her through the darkness.

'Run Morven, run!' he yelled. 'They've taken the McDuffs – we're the last... R*uuun.*'

The dreadful, piercing screams she heard coming from the direction of the entrance to the cave unnerved Morven. She tried to force her legs to move but they were rooted to the spot. As she struggled to move, a lightning bolt came hurtling towards her. It skimmed her shoulder, only just missing her head.

'How's that for starters?' howled Gretch with a hideous shriek of laughter, sending another assault of lightning bolts towards Morven.

Gretch was the daughter of Mogdred, the most evil and feared of all the Night Witches. But Mogdred had been blinded during her last battle against Lizzie the Protector and in order to guard herself from harm until her eyesight recovered, Mogdred had ordered that every Sea Dragon be killed. The reason for this is because Sea Dragons breathe out water which is so pure it can melt the black soul of a Night Witch, destroying it instantly.

Mounted on her broom, Gretch looked down gleefully as she swooped over the body of the male Sea Dragon. Her lightning bolt had made a direct hit. Mogdred would be pleased!

Gretch decided to land, but her huge stomach touched the ground before her feet could reach it, causing her broom to tip up at the back. The front dug into the ground like a javelin pole and sent her careering across the floor of the cave, wobbling like a jelly. When she finally stopped, she found it very hard to get back onto her feet. She had to roll onto her hands and knees, push her enormous bottom up in the air, then place each of her feet firmly on the ground, before managing to push up into a standing position.

Gretch was five feet tall, but her legs were only one foot long. They had shrunk down from carrying her enormous body around. She wore black tights and a black smock that barely covered her stomach. Her skin was such a dark shade of grey that it was almost black and on her face it hung down so much it looked as though it belonged to someone with a much bigger head. She had short black hair congealed with grease from never being washed and long hooked nails with ragged edges… good for ripping things apart!

Just as she entered the cave, Gretch's twin sister, Sloth, landed with a splat a few centimetres in front of her. A mirror image of Gretch, she too had been pole-vaulted off of her broom.

'Oi, watch out, you big lump!' Gretch complained.

'Oh, stop your whinging,' Sloth sniped back. 'We need to find the female Sea Dragon. C'mon, she can't be far away.'

The two sisters waddled into the cave side by side.

Gretch's first lightning bolt had acted like an adrenalin punch when it hit Morven, sending a rush of energy from her shoulder all the way down into her powerful legs. Although she couldn't see, at least she could move again.

Picturing in her mind a massive boulder that sat against the cave wall opposite her giant stone dining table, Morven ran straight towards it. As the tip of her nose made contact with the rock, she opened her jaws wide and blasted out a massive water jet. The boulder disintegrated immediately, revealing a secret exit. Tavish's last screams echoing in her head, Morven pushed through the large opening, spread her magnificent wings and disappeared beyond the clouds high above the cave.

Finding no more dragons in the cave, Sloth and Gretch soon grew bored and left to tell Mogdred all about how they had killed Tavish.

www.thumbletumble.co.uk
Find out more about this series, latest news, events and
when the next book will be available.

All books in the series can be ordered from the Thumble
Tumble website also available from your local bookshop
and online retailers.

www.scottishbookstore.com

Or by post from:
Thumble Tumble, PO Box 27132 Glasgow G3 9ER
Email:info@thumbletumble.co.uk

Follow the adventure!

Thumble Tumble and the Ollpheist is the first book in a series of eight.

Don't miss book two, *Thumble Tumble and the Cauldron of Undry*.

Look out for book three, *Thumble Tumble and the Eagalach Cup*, which tells how Thumble Tumble stumbles upon Mogdred's evil plan to attack the Thistle Pixies at the Eagalach Cup, and is hurtled into her most chilling adventure yet!

Completely unaware of the dangers, the feisty pixies prepare for their 'big game' with Thumble Tumble guarding them from the shadows. Follow her latest adventure as she eludes night walking Creepers and loathsome Tree Trolls on this incredible journey of discovery.

About the Author

A.H. Proctor is a successful businesswoman, wife and mother who has unashamedly lived in a fantasy world for most of her life. Captivated from childhood by fairy stories and the world of the Brothers Grimm, her fertile imagination was held in check until she took her own young children to the beautiful and mystical Isle of Arran. When, one day, they asked her to tell them a story of witches and dragons, the floodgates opened. Inevitably, Angela could not resist taking it a stage further and she began to write, and so the Thumble Tumble books set on mysterious Arran were born.